Arcemo

Tales From The World of Herta

♦

Arcemo Cloud Timeline (12th Era of Herta)

Table of Contents

Arcemo (Tales From The World Of Herta, #1) 1

Introduction 3

The Himortorian Map 5

The Seclouth Archeologist 19

Titles and Heroes 23

The Great Artifacter 29

The Hush'a'Moon Mountains 41

The Undergo Vault 49

The Lost Children 57

The Scorned 61

Gods of Herta So Far. 63

Note From The Author 65

A Short Biography About Me

Hey yo! My name is Haviti J. Washington! I am a humble young writer who loves many works of fiction and fantasy, creating fantastical stories set in places familiar and unfamiliar, known and unknown, a slice of life, or out of this world! I enjoy a great story when I can and I am quite cultured in pretty much all things. Ranging from the underrated characters in Marvel Universe, the latest model released from Games Workshop, and famous events happening with YouTubers. Like Markiplier or Preston! Not even Memes can escape my all-powerful gaze(Nanomachines, son!). I accept any form of constructive criticism, so please share your feedback on my latest works released and in the making. I live on the Big Island, calm and relaxing to me and perfect for a young writer beginning their writing journey for the first time. Of course, like always, everyone has their own personal opinions on what is considered *relaxing* to them or you. And that is what I strive for in my stories, what I consider to be, lacking in some sci-fi and fantasy books these days. And like a wise me once said: *Not everyone can become a Tolkien or Stephen King. But that doesn't mean that each person in the*

world shouldn't be uncreative or hold back their own unique story to tell everyone. Never forget that. Everyone has their own story to tell.

Introduction

Life is stranger than fiction. But that doesn't mean that fiction can't be strange in its own unique ways. For those of you who don't know, the strange worlds of fiction are as infinitely vast as our human imaginations, leaving us with endless stories that our conscious and subconscious manifest in our physical life here on Earth. Or shall I dare say, Herta. Yes, you read that quite right. It's Herta. At least, in a parrel universe from our very own that I may or may not have subconsciously created with my imagination during my naping hours on the family couch. It is on this blue little planet where history and mystery are pretty much one and the same as each other. Mythical beasts, ancient civilizations, origins of the universe, and of course, the debate on who was the first race that existed on Herta. Why? Dunno, makes your mind boggle, and think carefully about what could've happened that's why. Thinking first about something is better than talking now about what might happen. Again, think before you do. Always, no matter. Anyway, to give a brief summary of what this book is supposed to be. This book serves as an introduction to the fantasy world of Herta, the main characters that'll be lived in each era, and what role they served in the great continuity of Herta as a whole. Yes, the book is titled Arcemo. That's because the first beginning books will be covering short tales and stories surrounding her journeys alongside her friends across the continent of Wirm. Again, this book serves as an introduction to the world, just to clarify. In the world of Herta, especially on the continent of Wirm, where the Horned Race first discovered The Symbolic Tree, where the Knife Ears established the Silver Fortress, ever vigilant and ever standing in the face of the Red Valleys. It is here where the first race of Gorgmor founded the Kingdom of Arcanius, home to battlemages and supreme knights. It is also here, some would say, where a tremendous world-ending event will happen, where all who failed to worship Him and His ways, will suffer the infinite wrath of Yahmark, Divine Creator of All and Existence. Of course, only a few races, let alone small percentages of those races, actually believe in such. . . fairy tales. Fairy tales. A term that is used far too often for anything fantastical, supernatural, or better yet, unbelievable beyond imagination and comprehension. In short, is labeled immediately by the Artifactorium, as a myth or a fantasy, unless it was backed by concrete facts and truths, making it impossible to be a myth. Many great archeologists during the middle years of the Artifactorium, thought to believe that the Island of the Saidyk was said to be just a mere story spread by sun-crazed fishermen and sailors. . . until it wasn't. This caused many to question the reliability of the Artficatorium, for a brief amount of years that is. 1000 years have passed since the Island of Saidyk's official discovery, leaving much of the island's natives, the Sadyks, alone but aware of the outside world that surrounds them and ignores them. All of history though will forever change, when a loving, humble, 18-year-old Sadyk girl, one of her passions lying deeply in archeology and discovery, decides one day to join the glorified Artifactorium. . .

The Himortorian Map

"Beautiful." Heading into a new year, Lord Pickit smiled proudly upon his newly bloomed Romette flowers, sparkling and gleaming in the morning sun. Slowly sighing in comforting pleasure, he continued to sprinkle the clean water he just collected moments ago with his water can. Precisely, forty minutes ago, from the rain catcher system outside his porch. Some would question him why not just keep the flowers outside on the porch. It would certainly be much, much less of a hassle to maintain than to bring it out on a tightly run schedule. Fools, he would tell them so disdainfully. These were not just your ordinary garden variety roses you'll pick up from your local marketplace. These were Romette flowers, only blooming in the shade, and had a unique velvet color. Grown specifically for stuck-up lords such as himself, especially himself. Despite his rude demeanor and attitude toward his colleagues at the Artifactorium, he somehow managed to earn respect among a select few that knew him and his family's long contribution to the Artifactorium, mainly it being illustrious Artifacts and Overseers. Lord Odman Pickit had come upon these flowers as a congratulatory gift from his older sister since his first day on the job. His job as an Overseer wasn't all that hard compared to the fieldwork of an Archeologist. At least, to his personal opinion. In his father's words, managing others was easier than being managed yourself. Managing the Himortorian Culture branch for about five years straight and haven't run into any complications of any kind. He loved his role and his work in the Artifactorium, especially with the Himortian Culture hitting a personal place in his heart. Nothing could ruin this amazing moment he shared with his Romette flowers, peaceful and quiet, the massive courtyard below was still empty since it was still very early. Silence. . .he liked the silence. But like a battlemage's lightning bolt, his office door behind him shot open, behind it was a young Archeologist who answered Lord Pickit personally, finding hidden ruins and tombs, dating back to the

Old Kingdoms, two thousand millennia ago. The young Archeologist still had leftover dust and dirt from his most recent expedition outside Morvik City's walls, where he found what the lord was looking for. Lord Pickit sprang up from the sudden jumpscare, the water from his water can spurting all over his porch, he sighed annoyingly. He turned and saw mini dirt clods falling from his tangled mess of hair, along with red dust on his uniform. Lord Pickit honestly did not know how in all of Herta could someone like the Horians or the Horned Race could handle such extremities protruding out of their forehead. In other words, some of their horns grew upward, causing some unknowledgeable people to question if those things were uncomfortable or hindered them while they slept or when going through doorways. Other sub-races of the Horned Race have been shown to have a darker shade of green than the main race, while also having horns that were similar to rams and goats. Then again, who is someone like Lord Pickit, a human born from the House of Pickit, descended from the House of Pimon, to criticize a humanoid race that was around far longer than humans were, not to mention years ahead of technological achievements such as the Telesphere or Sandvox devices. But why was he here then? He must've found something for him to be this excited and frantic, for Lord Pickit knew that he wouldn't dare come back unless he found a certain something. This could only mean one thing and one thing alone.

"My lord! My lord!" Exclaimed the young Archeologist, who almost tripped on the way in to greet his superior. "I have the most wondrous news to tell you!"

"If you mean by *I found clues to the map of the hidden Himortorian Burial Sites*, then no, we have nothing to discuss, talk, converse, or anything of the sort." Lord Pickit placed his water can back on the porch front railing and nodded dramatically at his arrival. He sighed loudly, picked up the 12-inch pot, and placed the Romette flowers back on his office desk, aligning it with a miniature statue that resembled a knight from the Old Kingdom. "Now, now my delicate flowers. Now, now."

"Even better, my lord!" Swiping his backpack to his left arm, he rummaged through the multiple items he found on his most recent travels across the Kingdom of Melek, chuckling with excitement. "Even better!" From his backpack, dropped a small pickaxe tool that was spliced with a shovel of sorts. "Oh! Sorry, my lord! Hmmm. . ." He continued while Lord Pickit watched the objects that fell from his dirty backpack, raising a bushy eyebrow at his precarious behavior. "Aha! Here it is! The map to the hidden-"

Lord Pickit, in a catlike pounce, outstretched across his office desk, knocking over his miniature statue, and snatched the rolled paper map from the young archeologist, making him fall to the ground with a soft thud and a high-pitched gasp, no doubt the ironwood floor knocking him out on his trip down. Face meets the floor. "Yes! You found it! Finally. . . after all this time researching, spending countless nights awake, studying almost every treasured and legendary object in Himortorian history. The Himortorian colonizers, specifically those who came here left so many Artifacts. No doubt with their buried dead." Sitting in his chair, he unrolled the ancient-looking map with careful fingers, making sure not to rip or even so much as soil it. In his mind, it was a miracle that the map was even intact. Let alone survive that clumsy archeologist. Chuckling softly as the map was slowly revealed and flattened on his desk, its yellowed paper, smelling of flowers and pinewood. The unraveling aroma bombarded his office in a matter of seconds. Just like the historical documents read: Himotorians, when they first arrived on the coastal shores of Melek, made paper from the local trees they came across during their colonization of Melek. Yes, Himotorians had prior knowledge of the production of a paper press and various ways of distribution across great distances. This fascinated many historians and archeologists alike for their technological advancements. Sadly, the entire Himotorian race died out sometime during the Great Colonization, how they died is a mystery older than the Artifactorium itself, followed by loosely believed theories made by mad scholars. If he,

Lord Pickit, could discover an actual explanation for how and why the Himotorians died the way they did through the use of this map, not only would this upward his position in the Artifactorium but also finally gain recognition from his father, who he inspires his entire being from.

"Yes, yes. . .huh?" Lord Pickit's smile slowly faded when he finally noticed one tiny crucial detail on the map itself that is missing. The locations that were marked down were. . .completely erased, exact locations of the burial sites. "No! No, no, no! How can this be?" The lord peeked over his desk to where the unconscious archeologist was, the lord's face splat with anger. "You fool!" Proceeding to walk around his desk with large and loud footsteps, kicking the poor fellow in his left shoulder and saying to him. "Tell me, Bargas. . .did you find it as is or something had happened to it on your way here, to my office?" The kick was a bit much, but Bargas didn't mind. . .much. Even though Bargas had double the strength of a human, he always for some reason felt. . .powerless when in the presence of Lord Pickit. Not that Bargas was someone to have such feelings against his lord, especially anger or hatred towards him. For Bargas knew him to be quite infuriated from archeological dig to archeological dig, never once complaining to him about. . .pretty much. . .anything to be precise. "I found it that way, my lord." Raising himself from the floor, he dusted his uniform to meet eyes with the angered lord. "But I assure you it shouldn't be that big of an issue, once we give turn it into the Great Artifacter of cour-"

"No!" Lord Pickit exclaimed quietly. "Say nothing to the Great Artifacter. Nor anyone for that matter. Five years it took me to research the true value of Himortorian Artifacts and I will not allow for some old Highborn to take all the credit for it." The overcoat he wore swished left as he turned around and walked towards his chair, sitting and placing his hand in a thinking position. His eyes trailed to the map, sighing with disappointment. "The Great Artifacter already has a map of Himotorian burial sites across our good-hearted kingdom, showing the exact locations of some ancient corpses."

Bargas tilted his head in confusion at the lord's words. "If the Great Artifacter already has a map, why bother with all the secrecy? Surely he would just think that this is another burial site map from the Himotorian past. Right, my lord?" The Great Artifacter, known by all the archeologists who reside in the Artifactoirum, knows the man to be highly shrewd in all topics ranging from modern times to times that past and is in charge of categorizing and cataloging any Artifact across the continent of Wirm, storing them safely in the Undergo Vaults. Fixing his collar, Lord Pickit replied to Bargas swellingly, his gloved hands fidgety in the process. He looked outside to his porch once again, admiring the rueberry tree leaves that gracefully shifted in the cool spring breeze. "Not solely, my good Bargas. Not solely at all. The map that the Great Artifacter has currently, at this very given moment, is *a* map of Himotorian burial sites, however, it is not *the* map of the *hidden* Himotorian burial sites."

"Hidden as in. . ." Bargas waited for a quick reply, a dramatic answer to the awkward silence he forced upon himself. The lord stared at him, expecting him to know the answer. He sighed, sat up from his arched back, and tightened his gloves around his wrists. "The Himotorians were known to be one of the most technologically advanced civilizations the world has ever seen before the Great Colonization of Wirm, Bargas. When they died, so did their technological push on all of Herta suddenly ceased." Relaxing back deep into his chair, Lord Pickit could only dream of what the Himotorians could have been doing if hadn't gone extinct. "Wrist-sized devices that can manipulate the very fabric of the world, underground cities deep beneath Herta's skin, crimson metal giants that shaped entire mountains with their minds. If I could only find out where these hidden locations of the burial sites are on this map. . ."

"But you can't, my lord. Correct?" Bargas remembered what the lord said earlier about the missing details of the map, them being *unreadable*. "Because the words are-"

"Yes, it's because the words are. . ." Lord Pickit ceased in his reply, having a strange sensation that a familiar, horrible creature is advancing towards his office with lighthearted joy. A creature from a distant island, far, far away from the continent of Wirm. A creature so volatile in the lord's eyes, that it made him almost faint in fear of spontaneous destruction from just being in the same room with such a. . .creature. "Ohhh nooo. It's her." Lord Pickit was careful not to speak too loud for he knew the creature had better hearing than even a Knife Ear. "Quickly. Take. The. MAP." He mouthed the words while rolling the ancient map back into its original rolled form, frantically passing it to Bargas with haste. Nodding, he took the map quickly from the lords' hands, almost dropping it in mid-passing, placing it in a secure position in his backpack that he knew can't be crushed by the other tools and Artifacts he found out there. Good thing too he is wearing his protective gloves made of strich leather, making it nigh impossible to get his hands cut or injured from whatever unknown objects he found during his travels across the Kingdom of Melek in that backpack of his. "Quickly." Lord Pickit mouthed the words to Bargas once again, waving his arms and making hand gestures in the direction of his porch outside. "Go outside. Meet me underneath the clock tower when I call you from my Sandvox. It would most likely be around 11:00 SD(Sun Down), possibly two days from now if not more. In the meantime, attend to regular duties but most importantly of all. . .keep it secret and keep it safe. You understand me, Bargas?" Bargas bowed to his lord, Pickit immediately nodded and once signaled him to leave through his porch. He did this, making sure not to knock over any of the lord's potted plants he kept on the railings, dropping down silently with both his feet and darting across the recently trimmed grass of the Artifactoitum Center, making his way past the marbled columns and other doorways that led to schools and other offices, disappearing from Lord Pickit's sight when he turned to the dormitory spiraled stairs.

Now that the young lad was gone, he could finally prepare himself for the arrival of the islander. He picked his fallen miniature and re-aligned it with his Romette flowers, dusting off what dirt that was brought in by Bargas minutes ago. Veering his view to the left off to the side of one of his glass shelves, there stood a broom. Its wooden handle was engraved with strange symbols that lit up when he said. "Broom. Clean the floor over there." He pointed. With a whirring sound, followed by two poofs of the broom, hopping its way to the designated mess that it had been ordered to clean up. Voice magic some humans would say, but to the Artifactorium this is nothing more than a form of symbolic programming.

Readying himself for the oncoming storm, he reorganized his desk, placing papers and stacked documents making it seem like he was busy, cause if he didn't make it like he was doing something intricately important, he was going to be in for one massive talk from. . ."Blessed mornings to you, Lord Pickit!" Exclaimed the dark-skinned teenager as she opened the door, with an excited baby mugi beast walking by her side. The cute beast panted to sweat, so its saliva dripped every it went, and due to being half-dragon, it could breathe fire exactly like one. Well, sort of. A cone of fire burped out of its massive chompers, tongue licking its private part, similar to a small pug dog. The scaly-furred skin had an almost rainbow gleam about it when the scales reflected whatever light was in its surroundings.

He couldn't tell if the bloody thing was a male or female from where he sat observantly, acting like he was still reading a couple of documents that had information on the Knife Ear Kingdoms, their province, and the written history that they allowed sharing. "Mocho. No fire breath in Lord Pickit's office. Especially in the morning." Said the dark-skinned teenager gleefully, her gloved hands patting the beast on its heart-shaped forehead. Like a loyal pet, it listened to her without any fuss or resentment towards her, that being said, many mugi beasts tend to be quite rebellious towards their owners because they have the same thought process as their dragon ancestors.

But the beast wasn't the thing Lord Pickit was worried about at this very moment. It has been two months since her arrival and already she has found over forty Old Kingdom artifacts, many of them being Knife Ear and Gorgmor Era humans. Not to mention uncovering sixty-five ruins that date back also to the Gorgmor Era ironically, much of the ruins are mostly intact and covered by over fifty thousand years of build-up soil. The Newcomer some archeologists would call her. An outsider, a savage, a heathen, an island native, and for some weird apparent reason a practitioner of dark magic. Her name is Arcemo Cloud, a young, ambitious yet humble archeologist, who hailed from the Island of Saidyk.

"Lord Pickit sir!" Arcemo said, crossing her arms and bowing gracefully, half-excited, holding in what seemed to be a surprise. A surprise. Lord Pickit didn't mind surprises, as long as they didn't give him a heart attack. This, almost happened to him because Arcemo once brought him a small gift one Zoonday afternoon, wrapped in blue ti leaves, smelling like a sweet dessert.

Unfortunately for Lord Pickit, she had absolutely no idea that the purple potato treat would cause the lord to puff up such a storm, him being allergic and all. Then again, he had no idea he was allergic either.

"Good morning, Arcemo." He said with a pleasant voice, glancing at her with his eyes, then looked back to the paper he was *reading.* "How was your trip back from Bargera, Arcemo? I got the news that you came across cutthroats on your way back to the Artifactorium. Must've been quite terrifying, no. . .traumatizing for you to say the least. You sure you all right?" He asked, putting down the paper on the table, both hands flat and his furrowed eyes locked on Arcemo.

"Of course, my lord," Arcemo said. "We Sadyks have tough skins and an even tougher will to break. Besides, those bad people were scared silly by Mocho's mighty fire breath!" Laughing, she kneeled down and rubbed Mocho's scally cheeks. "That's right! You good Mocho boy. That's right! You are! You are!" Boy. Now he knew what the beast's gender is. Boy.

"Mocho, eh?" He looked at Mocho, leaned over his desk, and stretched out his hand as if he had treats in his hand or something, whistling and making clicking sounds with his tongue. "Hey. . . Mocho." Smelling hesitation and fear in Lord Pickit with curious eyes, Mocho began to lick his gloved hands, closing his reptilian eyes and slowly easing into his right palm, purring and calm. Tilting his head, this shocked Lord Pickit quite a bit. Most mugi beasts he met always tried to take a chomp out of him or blew fire at his face because their owners didn't discipline them enough, which in turn displeased the lord greatly.

"Good boy, Mocho." Arcemo clapped her hands together softly, her red eyes sparkling. "He's a good boy, my lord." He continued to rub Mocho on the head, a small smile forming on his middle-aged face, just from petting "I can definitely tell, Arcemo." He chuckled. "I must say Arcemo, your mugi is well trained! You must discipline him well, I suppose."

"It's more like I can understand what he says. He respects me and I respect him for what he is." She dusted off her mini purple skirt, which revealed most of her thick bare legs, most prominently from her thighs to her calves to her feet. Since she is Sadyk, her people naturally don't wear any type of *civilized* footwear or clothing for that matter, living on an island that is consistently bombarded by the glorious Great Suns. They wore purple loincloths made from their native Burgarto Water Bison. Also serving as a source of transportation, milk, and meat. Men were born with black hair while women were born with pink hair. All had red eyes, similar to certain sub-races of Knife Ears or their more complicated name the Kilvenderkrians. Yep, Knife Ears are fine, please.

But Arcemo was an educated girl, her parents, especially her father made sure of that. Educated to the point where she knew the main points in terms of how outsiders will react to her if she wore her native clothing.

So, from the many sea traders that came to the Island of Saidyk once a month every year, her father would trade rare crystals and a few of his own livestock, each time getting in return at least one piece of an archeologist's apparel and a stack of books covering many topics the 12 Eras of Herta.

Her father even taught her how to speak and write in the Ermaic tongue, which was the universal form of communication between the civilized races of Wirn, even though most civilized races preferred if they spoke in their own language. But like all Sadyk's, she quickly learned Ermaic with no effort and even wrote a few books documenting her island life and some Sadyk history that had been passed down by her ancestors.

"Oh." Lord Pickit said. "That. . .makes sense. You can understand. . .his tongue? You know, his language then? So, where is that bird that usually comes with you, Arcemo? The one that actually talks?"

"Bleak said she had to meet up with a dragon to discuss business." She nodded in confirmation to his question, making him lean back into his chair with a face of understanding, with her creature Mocho crawling back to her and wrapping his tail around the base of her thick feet, resting its scally under the chin on them. Breathing slowly and relaxed, knowing his good friend Arcemo is safe and sound, sensing no danger or intent of danger towards her. In Arcemo's hand, she held a rectangular letter, a green wax seal that had Lord Pickit's family symbol, the Flying Betta Fish. This could only mean that someone back at his family estate(The Pickit Manor) had sent a letter of great importance to him. How exciting! He pondered who it must've been to send him a letter, which it could have been anyone who is still living back at the family manor, the particular individuals being his mother, sister, first cousin, second cousin, father's brother, mother's sister or his sister's husband. Which is Newt. Just Newt. Literally just Newt. No fancy last name, family name, or even an honorary title for a heroic deed he had done for any known kingdom, specifically the Kingdom of Orthor or more commonly referred to as *Orthane* in the Knife Ear's language. Oh, yes. He is also a Knife Ear or at least a sub-race of the elegant Knife Ears, more rugged and country-like, comfortable living within the many, many thick forests of Wirm.

It's not that he disliked her sister's choice of a husband. . .much. But if he had to be honest with his sister(Which to be fair, wasn't very often.), her being the firstborn child, she had, to say the least, interesting cemented standards when it came to her visage of a perfect husband, having an actual written down list. These were as followed:

- ***He must be mysterious with not only himself but also with everyone he converses with daily.***

- ***Has a nicely grown beard, nothing too bushy and nothing too goatee-looking. Rugged, even.***

- ***Skilled with the sword and bow, but not like a knight from the Kingdom of Arcanius.***

- ***He always tells the good, honest truth like how all people should in this world.***

Lord Pickit even had the great honor of listening to his sister always quoting these very standards in front of him when he was only 12 years old. Every single day, sometime around 5:00 SU to 8:00 SD But it's his older sister for crying out loud. It wasn't his business to meddle with someone else's choice of a husband. Especially his sister. He was brave but not that brave. His main strength was his cunning personality and the manipulative nature of others of lower demeanor and stature.

No matter how hard he tried though, trying every single tactic he has ever used to get his way, nothing worked on Arcemo. The girl simply helped around the Artifactorium as much as she could, assisting important figures across this vast school built over one of the first archaeological sites of the 10th Era that guided generations of constructive knowledge, ultimately for the betterment of all races. The individuals she assisted most of the time were the Librarian, the Great Artifacter, Highlord Aegrik, and even the famous monster slayer Uldric Surefellow, half-human and half-Knife Ear.

Even now, all she wanted to do to assist the lord today was by fetching his mail. Simple as that. "Is that the mail, Arcemo?" Lord Pickit asked. "Yes, it is my lord. Must be from your family too, it has the green symbol and everything." With two steps closer to his desk, she handed him the letter, putting both of her hands behind her back, rocking herself back and forth on her bare heels. Her expression was both alluring and calming to say the least, keeping a bright smile as if she knew everything was going to be swell for the rest of the day. Her red colored eyes closed and her head tilted slightly to the left, continuing to rock back and forth, saying to him."Before I go, I just wanted to congratulate you, my lord."

The letter in hand, he opened a drawer, and out came a small letter opener, the silver handle designed with a raven head as its pommel. He lifted an eyebrow, his attention still locked on the letter he was trying to open. "Congratulate me, you say?" Like an explosive spell, she jumped in the air and shouted. "Happy Artifact Day!" Jumping from the chair slightly, dropping his letter opener on the wooden floor, holding the cut-open letter close to his chest. Lord Pickit's surprised eyes stared long at the cute Sadyk girl. Then Arcemo continued, "Happy Artifact Day?" He hesitantly said."That's not. . .wait, it's today?!? Please tell me it's not today, Arcemo." Nodding up and down happily, she said. "Yep! I mean, it's today I suppose! Everyone kept saying it to me before they speedily went off to do their business. What is Artifact Day?" She asked curiously.

"Oh. . ." He seems relaxed now, releasing today wasn't *his* Artifact Day. "It's a holiday, to celebrate the first artifact you found when you join the Artifactorium. The day you celebrate Artifact Day is the same day you found your first artifact. Say, you found a Gorgmorian artifact-"

She perked up when she heard him say this. "I found about 14!" With a slow nod of his head, he knew that the young Sadyk found a multitude of fantastic artifacts. Arcemo Cloud is the youngest archaeologist to join the Artifactorium in history. The only Sadyk in . . .history to be exact.

Many people who lived in Morvick City, found it quite. . .odd. For the Sadyk, a race that rarely interacted with any of the races who lived on the continent of Wirm, just one day send a single Sadyk girl, who had extensive knowledge of the Old and New Kingdoms, suddenly came out of the blue and joined the Artifcatorium. Odd, too many. But not to Lord Pickit, no he never thought anything suspicious of her at all.

In his eyes, he saw a young archeologist. A fellow historian. A *kind* person. Something the Artifactorium needed more often. Granted, he may have tried to manipulate her in her beginning days(Which wasn't successful at all.), but over time he kinda grew on her whole being, her personality, her very nature. But he could only tolerate so much of her these days.

"Yes, yes, 14 of them. I remember." He said quickly. "Is that all you wanted to tell me, Arcemo?" He grabbed the cut-opened envelope and took it out, unfolding the letter to see the written message for him and him only.

"Yep, that's all, my lord." Arcemo said brightly. Crouching down to Mocho, patting the top of her thighs, and said. "Come on, Mocho! Let's go." Standing up with a warm smile, she walked toward his office door and opened it, letting chubby Mocho go first and make his way down the hallway. Before she left, she turned her head, her sparkling pink hair swerving as she did so, bowed joyfully, and smiled. "Blessed mornings to you once again, Lord Pickit."

Arcemo closed the door behind her, prancing along with her bare feet in the long hallway, Mocho in front with his chin held high while they left. She was gone, finally. He was alone at last, leaving only himself to bother, and luckily, he is incapable of bothering himself. "Now," Lord Pickit said, unfolding the letter entirely, revealing the carefully written words. "Let's see who writing to me." His eyes scanned the paper, from a relaxed to a concerned expression. It read:

Dearest son, I have heard the recent news of your successful position up in the Artifactorium. Good for you! Your sister told me all about it. However, I can't say I will be attending your celebration day for sure, due to the numerous Giant attacks in the Southern Territories of the Horned Race Kingdom. And as a Supreme Knight, whose sole responsibility is to protect the good people of Wirm and uphold the image of True Peace, I might be here for another week or so. Please, don't be mad at me. I know haven't been able to attend well, any of your Artifact Days since your joining, and for that, I am truly sorry. But as a father, the first chance I get to finally leave this campaign, I will. I can never promise but I will try my very best to get back home to you all before you can say I found it! I love you son and I hope to see you again.

Father

The room fell silent as the ill expression lord fell back into his chair, his face almost dead looking. He then closed his eyes, inhaled deeply, and exhaled with a shudder. The tree's leaves blew softly in the morning breeze, the current time of the day now being 7:45 S.U. "I found it." Lord Pickit said quietly. "I guess."

The Seclouth Archeologist

"It has been a good 5 months since her arrival and already she has brought more Artifacts in than any of us could even imagine. Seriously, I have been keeping watchful eyes on her and have yet to confirm if she has done anything related to Dark Magic, communicating with evil spirits and creepy, eerie entities. I will prove her wrongdoings by any *good* means possible. Now, are you in or not?" Jorka said, sitting on a chair, resting her arms on the large circular library table, other young archeologists reading informational books on different histories across the continent of Wirm, the majority of the books they read covered the 3rd Era or 4th Era of Herta when war was a very, very prominent thing in the lands. Some archeologists glanced at what Jorka, a female Horian archeologist, was saying about the Sadyk girl known as Arcemo Cloud.

"No. No-why are you even talking to me about this, Jorka?!" Mirk said. His elongated ears twitched from hearing such accusations, realigning his glasses so they met his eyes and were resting on the bridge of his nose. "Look, there may be many accusations towards her because she seems *suspicious*. But honestly, I really don't see her being a user of Darkness. Trust me, I have seen many individuals who have fallen to Dark Magic. Arcemo is not one of them. Besides, she couldn't be a user of the Darkness, otherwise, the Great Artifacter would have known by now, don't you think?"

"Maybe she somehow found a way to conceal-" He quickly interrupted Jorka to ensure his point.

"To conceal her Dark Magic from the Great Arifacter. You do know how ridiculous that sounds, right?" A long pause came between the two archeologists. Jorka rubbed her horns in annoyance at the Knife Ear's superior knowledge. He then continued, closing his notebook."Do not forget, dear Jorka, that the Great Artifacter is a Highborn human. Highborns have two primary abilities that give them their superior place among other humans descended from Gorgmor. They can detect any form of Darkness and can also destroy any form of evil if needed. If Arcemo is *evil,* she wouldn't even be alive now, would she?"

She sighed loudly, face palmed herself, and grunted. "I hate it when your right," Jorka said, lifting her head, her eyes in a pondering position. "But still, you never know. Maybe. . ."

"Maybe what, Jorka?" Questioned Mirk, raising his large glasses back to his eyes.

"Maybe the Great Artifacter has been *corrupted* by the Darkness. He spends most of his time in his tower reading about Artifacts of terrible power during the 1st Era of Herta. Strange, right?"

"You sound crazy, you know that?" Mirk nodded in disagreement, opening his notebook and attending to a rough sketch of some female figure. Wide hips and some meat on her body, not fat but more to the chubby side. He hardened a few lines surrounding the empty face. "Undeniably crazy."

She raised an eyebrow at whatever he was drawing, piquing her rock-blasting curiosity. Jorka snatched so fast from his hands that it left him dumbfounded and mildly angry at her for doing something childish. Both were only 20 years old. Both had their wants and dreams. Both had their own little. . .*pleasures.* Mirk scoffed softly, looked up at Jorka, placed his pencil on the table, and said. "Give it back, Jorka. Please."

"Well, what is this? I didn't know Knife Ears had a thing for drawing *girls.*" Giving a small smirk, flipping through the multiple pages. Most of them contain sketches of chubby girls and personally written notes of his daily experiences at the Artifactorium. Most of them being about his own archeological finds the past two years. "Ooh, this one here looks wild. Here, I thought Knife Ears were all supposed to be elegant."

"For your information, not all Knife Ears have the same goals and ideals. Of course, we all believe in a greater good and True Peace, but it doesn't mean we all like the same type of you-know-what." Mirk, despite being a Knife Ear, grew heavily impatient about her possession of his belonging. "Now please, give back my notebook."

She chuckled in his growing anger and said. "Alright, alright, I just wanted to fool around. . ." She held her last words as a certain page caught her Horian eyes. This page in particular had a very familiar person on it. One who lived in the Artifactorium. It was the Sadyk girl, drawn in a sitting position facing a window, the sun's light shining through her face. She held one knee up close to her chest, her bare feet unshifted from the square cushion she sat on. Jorka raised both eyebrows raised in this shocking revelation. Her eyes were now on Mirk, his cheeks turning red as if he knew what she was looking at. "Mirk."

"What?" Mirk said, with annoyance in his voice.

"I didn't know you had a thing for Arcemo." A devious smile formed on her face. "You like her."

With a sharp grunt, he took back his notebook from Jorka's hands and stuffed it into one of his coat's inner pockets. "Yeah, I like her. So what?" Mirk said sharply. "Unlike most girls, I met in Morvick City, Arcemo Cloud is what I would consider. . .*seclouth*."

Jorka was left confused. "Seclouth?"

"Yeah, seclouth. She's. . .strange and unusual to me. A rare beauty. A hidden gem." Mirk said quietly. "That's seclouth."

Jorka scoffed and continued to read her book titled: *A Contemplative Collection of the History of the **Scorned***. "You just like her because she's a Sadyk girl. I mean come on, when do you see a girl with naturally pink hair? Like never, pray I tell you."

Once again, he nodded with a face of disagreement. "You suck, you know that, Jorka. You suck."

Titles and Heroes

"Haven't you heard, dear brother of mine?" Said Sulrick the Masher.

"What? What haven't I heard, Sulrick?" Replied Aven Demer.

"I am getting a new title soon, dear brother of mine! Isn't that great or terrific or fantastic, no funtastical news to hear?!?!" Smiling excitingly, jumping up and down, the holstered steel club moving with the armor's movement.

"Stop that jumping you doing! You are not a child. Okay, I'll admit you are not that bright when it comes to being a young adult." The few words he said after were under his voice. "Despite you being 4 years older than myself."

"Aren't you happy?" Sulrick questioned. "I mean, I'm getting a new title and everything, dear brother of mine. Instead of mashing, I am crushing now!"

"It's not that, Sulrick. It's the fact you think having a title is better than being a hero of the people. Even a child could know the difference."

"Alright, then, dear brother of mine." Pouted Suldrick, dusting off a nearby bench and sitting on it loudly, tapping the iron boots together. Scoffed and said. "If you are so smart, why don't you tell me why being a hero is better than having an awesome title such as mine."

Crossing his arms, his steel bracers clinking one another. "Alright, I'll explain. I'll explain clearly to ya too, so you can understand and remember it." Said Aven Demer, sitting down next to his sibling, exhaling with tired shoulders. Whipping out a smoke pipe, carved from a trunk of pine wood. He banged, cleaning it out with a slender small black stone, a cleaning tool simply. Blowing through his pipe, excess charred B'marg weed, which was a certain brand that heroes like Aven had a certain taste for over time. "Remember the tale of the Timeless Knights?" His pipe was at the corner of his mouth when he spoke.

"Hmmmmm. . ." Pondering long and hard, until Sulrick finally said. "No. I think forgot about it a while ago back when I got hammered in the head by vicious bandits who were pillaging a small fishing village. Do tell more, dear brother of mine."

"I will tell you, Sulrick but I will also try to forget about the head hitting and all of that." Aven blew harder through his smoke pipe loudly, a few shriveled bits of weed left, then said. "Sit back, sit tight, and enjoy the short story of the Timeless Knights."

The Tale of the Timeless Knights

Written by Nirt Frenry III during the 3rd Era, a supposed Knife Ear survivor of the Infinite Wars and actual witness of the Timeless Knights

Before the discovery of True Peace

War plagued the good lands of Wirm

Good people turn on each other

From the Madness that unfolded before them

The Users of Dark Magic, their spells caused the Great Shadow

The end seemed to be near for all

I, Nirt Frenry III, a Knife Ear soldier who served over 40 campaigns

Having only a simple title and a honed blade of magnificence

I have witnessed, the Timeless Knights

True Heroes I say, True Heroes

Appearing from nowhere, us with no knowledge of who or where they came from

Told us all that they represented our common ideologies

Specifically, for all the good people of Wirm

But to do so, they said

One must fight the other

Knight against knight against knight

Each took the form of a race we knew

Knife Ear, Horned and Gorgmorian

Told us that with their sacrifice, the Great Shadow will vanish

They said it was Yahmark's will

So did the TImeless Knights fight each other

Weapons clashed, clearing the dark skies
Battle cries, the stars shifted
In their final hours, they became First Constellations
So ended the Great Shadow, Devourer of Existence
So continued the Infinite Wars, race against race
War consumes but True Peace creates
Titles come and go from era to era
But no one will ever forget a True Hero

"So," Aven said, puffing a few mini clouds of smoke in the air. "Now do you understand **why**? Why being a true hero is far better than being a person with a fancy title that might not mean **anything**? What do you truly **stand** for? What you truly are to the good people of Wirm?" Aven waved around his smoke pipe in the air as he talked, trying to exaggerate the point he was trying to make. "Well, what say **you**?"

"Hmmm. . ." Sulrick thought long and hard about what the tale meant and symbolized. Because every tale had a hidden meaning behind it, some literal and some not. "I *guess* understand, dear brother of mine."

"You guess?" Aven said bluntly, the puffs ceasing from his pipe. "You guess?! I suppose you didn't understand a single part of the story then, eh?"

"Well, actually. . ." Sulrick began slowly, until from the lily pad gardens behind them, a young archeologist Sadyk girl, by the name of Arcemo Cloud. The two knew her since her arrival and already she discovered more lost knowledge than any newly joined archeologist who studied beforehand for 5 years or so. She didn't know, but the lily pad ponds were **not** meant to be walked into. To her, the ponds here at the Artifactorium looked similar to the ones back home, where they were used as feet relaxers or Soothing Ponds.

"Oooh, these soothing ponds are nice!" Arcemo chirped happily to herself while walking through the pond behind the bench Aven and Sulrick were sitting on. They looked at each other first, with raised eyebrows and slanted mouths. They didn't mind her, because most of the people here that's pretty much irritated daily by talking about themselves and what they found today. But not Arcemo, oh no. Like all Sadyks, they're completely incapable of annoying a person. They're just too kind.

"It's her." They mouthed in unison. When reading up on the Sadyk race, it is said that their hearing is better than some animals on Wirm, specifically elephants.

Lifting one foot while balancing on the other, outstretching her toes and wiggling them, sighing with comfort in her voice. She turned her head and smiled at both Aven and Sulrick, bowing her head at the same time. "Blessed mornings to you both, friends," Arcemo said brightly. "I was just rinsing my feet real quick. I mean, I did travel through Moriman Forest and back. Plenty of mud and stuff."

Aven nodded, puffing a few from his pipe."You don't say, Arcemo. You don't say. Hmm. . .I heard you Sadyks are quite resilient when it comes to terrain and all, right? I mean, your skin is stronger than pure steel for crying out loud."

"Well, we Sadyk's live on an island in the center of *Usablu,* or the Virsirmir Ocean you call it, that is constantly bombarded by the Great Suns. We Sadyks call them *Hjiu.* I think that might have something to do with my people." Arcemo said politely, walking out of the pond with wet footsteps on the stone floor and flicking whatever remaining water she had on her feet. Outstrecthing her arms fully and yawned softly, then rubbed her right eye in tiredness. "I'm off to eat some breakfast, now."

"See you later today, Arcemo," Aven said happily, tilting his head with a small nod. "You'll most likely find me and Sulrick at the front entrance of the Artifactorium, talking and whatnot, okay?"

"We always enjoy a good chat from you, Arcemo." Sulrick said while leaning back on the bench. "If you ever need some smas-I mean crushing to do, I'm always here, dear friend of mine!"

"Okekdokey!"Picking up her backpack, slouching it over her shoulder, and skipped through the marbled hallways of the Artifactorium, heading to the cafeteria most likely. Humming a native tune while she did so, feeling happier and happier with every step she took. "See you later!"

The Great Artifacter

All kingdoms across the continent of WIrm knew the importance of the Artifactorium's main goal and purpose. Publicly, the betterment of Wirm and safeguarding of lost knowledge. Then again, that was for the *public* to know. And the Great Artifacter knew this all too well what the true intentions of the Artifactorium. Specifically, the **Head Artifactium**, who is the leaders of the Artfactorium, their names alone were something to fear, although only a rare few even knew their true names. Still, it's not that he was fearful or anything of the **Head Artifactium**, just mutual respect between him and them. Mutual respect. An occasional talk back here or maybe even a slight argument that could have escalated into some unneeded nonsense. It's not that the Great Artifacter was disliked by the **Head Artifactium**, nor was he considered a disruptor of historical knowledge of Wirm. Many considered him and his Highborn relatives. . .*unusual*. Especially the **Head Artifactium**. Like the island people, the Sadyks, for example. Even though many archaeologists consider him bonkers mad, many other archeologists consider him a figure of inspiration. After all, he once was one some years ago. An archaeologist. But with great age, especially being around 87 years old, it was about time he slowed down. Nowadays, he spends his trivial mornings and afternoons in the Blue Spire, being a philosophizer, a mathematician, a great inventor, a renowned historian, and an ecstatic teacher. A teacher who listens and understands his students. These were his drifting thoughts of the Great Artifacter when he was up in his tower, looking at old books and scrolls dating back to long-lost cultures and ancient people. Besides, being banned from archeology entirely after the Chantel Incident, the Great Artfacter needed to occupy his mind somehow during his old age. Yes, Highborns can live far longer than the average descendant of Gorgmorian humans, ranging from 200 to 600 years of age. That's just historically known too. Highborns came from the Island of Vigoria, a lush green, tropical island of magnificent blue sand, smooth giant sandstone castles, and yes, of course, sand dragons. In the Blue Spire, much of the inner furnishings and furniture were made to be similar to his homeland. Tables, chairs, rugs, and all. Today though, the time is 9:00 SU(Sun Up), in the midsection of the Blue Spire, where 24 windows built in an up, down, up, down motion shined sunlight in the morning. Here in the mid-section, students and young archeologists, mainly ones in their very early 20s, were able to eat their breakfast during their classroom studies in front of the Great Artifacter. He didn't mind, why would he? In fact, most mornings in the circular classroom, he would occasionally share some of his Morning Share Pie, blueberry special too. Cutting them perfectly to the point where it was practically a magic show, amazing to the eye. The Great Artifacter now had about three students/ archeologists, with a third on her way. Page through pages, he flipped through a book titled: *Forgoon Age: <u>Believed</u> or <u>Not Believed</u>?* It wasn't his book, it was a student's checked-out book. Jorka Jamba to be precise. He raised an eyebrow, streaking his gray hair back a couple of times, and hummed a random melody from his homeland.

"Well, Jorka." He commented funnily. "Sorry to ruin your breakfast but as a once full-time archeologist, one who *has* traveled across half the continent and discovered known archeological finds of your time, I can safely say that the Forgoons are very, very extinct. Besides, their civilization seems very uh. . .standoffish maybe? Also, some of the things they supposedly built. Sounds like fiction to me. Very much like fiction."

Jorka made a groaning sound of disappointment, her mouth stuffed and lips messy with Morning Share Pie, she spoke with food in her mouth. "What part sounds like fiction to you, my lord?"

"Everything." He said bluntly. "Mainly in chapter four, mentioning something about star camps hovering above the skyline and traveling among the many constellations with metal ships. Sounds a lot like the Himortorians of old. Giant metal ships and floating star castles. From a realistic viewpoint, all this technology could only be possible if well. . ."

"If well *what*, my lord?" Jorka said respectfully, swallowing what pie was left and scratching the base of her left horn.

A big smile formed on his face."Well. . .if the **Absolutes** were around of course."

"Ooh, I heard of the **Absolutes**, my lord!" Mirk Basilva commented loudly, already finished with his boiled eggs and steamed rice. Reading a book on one of the Great Arfacter's favorite subjects: *The First Era of Herta: Why is it not talked about enough?* "They were godlike beings who were responsible for the creation of Wirm, existing before the 1st Era of Herta."

"Not godlike, young Mirk." He said. "Not godlike at all. In fact, godlike means *like a god*, and from what recorded history says, they are gods. They existed at the Birth of Existence when Yahmark or Yahmen created the First Light, assisting him in creating all of Existence, including the universe, Wirm, and the neighboring planets that we can see from our telescopes. Wirm is also the center of the universe, not the sun. Those who believe that the sun is the center of our good universe are either stupid or they are some sun-worshiping moronic cultists."

All the young archeologists giggled quietly in the classroom, the two boys being the most prominent. Then behind Mirk's chair, Bargas asked. "That's another thing, my lord, that I wanted to ask."

The Great Artifacter scanned the classroom to see Bargas, who was kinda hiding behind Mirk, shy and scared looking. "When a person speaks, they should speak with a sure and wise voice. So, Bargas, what is it you wanted to ask?"

Bargas shrugged his shoulders funnily and said. "The Himortorian race. Why are their *artifacts* so important to, you know, the Allied Kingdoms and all? Why are they? I just need to understand that's why, my lord."

The Great Artifacter seemed all a bit. . .puzzled. Unlike the supposed Forgoon, The Himortorians were a race that once existed before any of the main races developed vast kingdoms. A lot of the main races, excluding the Knife Ears, were nothing more than simple tribes. In fact, there is actual evidence that they had a global footprint upon all of Herta, leaving behind many, many ruins of their mysterious ancient civilization.

The Great Artifacter closed the book and placed it upon a tall stack behind him. The other archeologists looked at Bargas, all of them kinda confused why would he ask this. Everyone knew he studied the Himortorian culture quite extensively. Why ask now? He sat quietly, swerving his study chair slowly in the direction of one of many colored-glass windows. "Whether any of you like to believe it or not, the world around us is. . .old. Very old. Older than any of known race to be clear, Bargas."

"Older than even elegant Knife Ears, eh, my lord?" Jorka made a pointing gesture toward Mirk, almost in a teasing manner. He squinted his eyes and stuck his tongue out in an instant retaliation.

"Yes, Jorka." The Great Artifacter turned to face his classroom, the sunlight shining half of his face, the other shadowed in darkness. "Even older than the Knife Ears. If I remember, I think the plants were one of the first things that were created on Herta. You'd be surprised what natural secrets our world, Herta, has in stock for all of us. The Himotorians. . .well, let's just say that many of the things they built were used for. . .*unnatural* things. So, if any of you come across Himotorian artifacts in any of your expeditions, I'd advise you immediately go to your teachers, so they can lock them up in the Undergo Vault."

Everyone fell silent at his words, truthful yet full of mystery. They knew that what he was telling them was not to be taken lightly, at all. They nodded their heads to the Highborn lord until Jorka broke the silence by saying.

"Well, life is stranger than fiction. . .I guess. Anyhow, don't mind me everyone 'cause I'm going to take a sip from my favorite river water-AHHH!" Jorka said as she reached for the glass water bottle on the corner of her desk, letting out a short scream as she watched fall to the floor and ear-piercingly shattered. Pouted lips and a sad groan, Jorka couldn't help but feel sick at the thought of the river water she wasted. Purified too.

"Gods damn it!" Jorka exclaimed with annoyance. "Ugh! That was my last bottle too! Don't worry, my lord, I'll clean it up right n-"

"Blessed mornings to you all!" Arcemo gleefully announced herself as she entered the classroom from behind Jorka's chair and desk, halfway to the glassy mess on the floor, Jorka didn't recognize the *familiar* voice that said this to all of them. Nor did she bother to warn the person that unknowingly proceeded toward the shattered glass. Everyone looked at Arcemo, then looked at Jorka.

His ears twitching, Bargas shouted. "Arcemo, the floor!" Almost jumping from his seat, Bargas had forgotten much of the written history of the Sadyk race, lifestyle, and their *unique* durability. Cause naturally, a regular person would feel excruciating pain if they walked barefooted on broken glass, much less why or how the person steps on said broken glass in the first place.

"Hmm?" She said, then with one foot over the broken glass, her arms wrapped around three books and. . ."Huh? Oh. Did you drop your water bottle, Jorka? Here. You can take mine, then!" Arcemo had her left barefoot on the glass, unfazed and unharmed. Luckily though for Jorka, Arcemo always carried a sufficient amount of water on herself at all times. She carried them in her backpack.

Jorka however, was greatly disappointed and astounded by this newfound surprise. All her horned life, she always thought that the supposed tales of Sadyks skin being harder than iron, steel, and even some cases dragon scales, were all myths and fairy tales. Just to keep children entertained and in school. Jorka couldn't conceal her scoff and a rude reply. Not to mention how she yanked the water bottle from Arcemo's hand.

"Thanks. . .I *guess.*" Jorka said as sat back on her chair, tapping her boot against the stone tile floor and acting as if nothing happened, resting her chin in her closed fist, blowing away the strands of hair that blocked her eyes. In her mind, she said, *Here I thought that was going to be one heck of a laugh today. Huh. Guess not.*

Arcemo, knowing how Jorka felt toward her at the moment, retracted her hand normally as ever and closed her backpack. Not that many people on Wirm know this, but Sadyks are very, very emotional people. Their control over their emotions allows them to concentrate on thorough difficult times like long-term arguments. Sure, among the Knife Ears race, there are some powerful empaths in their own right but how Sadyks handled their emotions was. . .a little weird to say the least. Even so, she still kept that same soft smile she always had on most of the time, nodded to Jorka, and walked to her desk. Before Arcemo sat, she remembered that the *borrowed* books were to be returned to the Great Artfacter today.

"Here you are, my lord! All three books I borrowed yesterday." Arcemo said. "I must say good lord, there is a lot more history about Wirm I had no idea about. It's baffling, to say the least. Symbolic programming, ancient civilizations, and even gods. Gods, good lord! Even though I don't believe in a whole pantheon of gods, I still find them so incredible to read about. By Usami, I love history. I love archeology too, good lord!"

He couldn't help but smile at how she acted around others, for there is a very few young people who join the Artifactorium that actually have that same passionate drive in their careers. Recently of late, he's been hearing multiple other students rambling on and on about secret treasures, untold power awaiting them, and soon-to-be royals. Nonsense he would say, a bunch of it. Like his father used to say, *If you're young, you're young. Don't waste your youth by doing foolish acts. You'll live to regret them.* But Arcemo was one of the few that actually carried that passion for what she truly loved to do in her career. It shows in her work too. In everything, she did really. Even her upbeat Sadyk spirit brought a new feel when she first arrived at the Artifactorium. Day One. "I'm glad to hear that, Arcemo. I am glad to hear that. True passion for what you seek to do in life is always important. Never let anyone tell you or any of your friends otherwise."

"I will remember your wise words forever, my lord. You truly are the Great Artifacter! Only. . ." Arcemo paused, positioned both of her feet inward slightly, rubbing both hands together shyly. "I. . . don't really have that much friends at the moment, my lord. Still, wise words nonetheless."

Bursting out in laughter, Jorka looked at Arcemo with contempt. "Ahh, that's too bad." Not bothering to keep herself in check, Jorka couldn't keep in the inner jealousy and sass she had toward the Sadyk girl. "Considering you come from an island, bustling with social activity amongst *your* kind, I thought you'd be good at making friends. I wonder why."

Bargas laughed. "Don't listen to her. I think people just got warm up to you Arcemo. Unlike you, Jorka, who gets ridiculed because of your disproportionate horn growth. At least mine grow normally."

"No one asked you, Bargas!" Swerving her torso in the direction of Bargas, staring at him intently. "And who around here ridicules me? Hmm? Who does? No one dares-"

"SILENCE! Both of you." Mirk threw crumpled pieces of paper directly at their heads, both Jorka and Bargas grunting from his precise aiming. "The Great Artifacter has *that* face again." He said in a quiet singsong fashion. This caught both their attention of course as if the paper balls hitting their heads weren't enough as it is. They turned to see the Great Artifacter's face completely. . .blank, looking down at his desk as if something was. . .worrying him very, very deeply. They barely saw him like this, since he was a very uppity old man, who cared for the youngster around the Artifactorium as if they were his own grandchildren. And for them to see him worry, made them worry. Even Arcemo, who stood right in front of his desk, stared innocently at him with curious eyes. Tilting her head to the side, she spoke.

"My lord?" Arcemo could feel that he. . .sensed something or someone nearby that gave him this bearing look on his face. His frow wrinkled, blinking as if his attention just got caught on by an unwavering bird flying past his sight or a jumping squalker fish leaping out of its large pond.

"Ah. . ." He held his words and made a slow, tightening fist. Then smile before he continued. "Hmm. Well my students, sorry but there will be no lesson today! I just remembered I have someone important dropping off a special package for me. As you all should know, I like my **privacy** when it comes to **privacy**. And as any archeologist should know is-"

"That privacy is the only place one can concentrate on a certain something!" All his students joyfully said in unison. Jorka intentionally swayed her head as she said so to everyone. Her eyes were still locked on Arcemo, still suspicious of her entire being, she thought to herself: *Smile while you can, Sadyk. I'll prove to everyone you are not what you say you are. Mark my words, Sadyk. Mark my words, Arcemo Cloud.*

An hour has passed since his students left his classroom quietly, leaving him to himself and an unknown arriving visitor very, very soon. Yes, he told them that he was receiving a *package* today for his students as a cover story. But in reality, he had no idea who this person was that speedily walked faster and faster towards his office. This unknown person was definitely humanoid but in no guarantee either Knife Ear or Horned folk. Maybe a Ultr'mite? A Saumar? Perhaps even another Sadyk maybe. No. No, the aura this humanoid had, for some odd reason completely oblivious to the Great Artifacter, something similar to his own. Another Highborn. . .possibly but highly unlikely. Highborns tend to, ironically, stay away from each other at all times if possible. The main Highborn families particularly stayed away from each other most of the time. If this was a Highborn, why would he or she come to the Great Artifacter, an senile, old Highborn who spent the rest of his years serving the good people of Wirm, through his teachings and the knowledge he had learned throughout his life. Closer and closer, the mysterious person approaches the doors and opened them violently to the point where they both banged the walls behind them. Unafraid of this armored person, the hood shrouding the face, he asked first who this person was and why was he or she there for. The person seemed to just examine the surrounding classroom, the colored window panes, and of course, the Great Artifacter sitting at his half-circled desk. A smile grew on his face as the mysterious person who walked towards his desk, started to feel strangely. . .familar. The Great Artifacter chuckled.

"I've seen many dramatic entrances in my life. But that was absolutely terrible. . ." The Great Artifacter began. "Little brother."

Resting his hands on his hips, a rumpus laugh came from his voice. With his left, he flicked two fingers and in an instant, his hood vanish magically without a trace. His armor, once black, turned a magnificent light purple and at his back a short cape formed, sparkling from the sunlight that shined in. The Great Artifacter got up from his chair and hugged his little brother tightly. Exhaling his breath, patting him on his back happily.

"Good to see you again, Malkai, my brother!" Shormai shouted excitedly. "I can't believe my magic actually worked this time! It took me forty moons to master it and hold the aura for longer than 4 minutes."

"Only a true, good-hearted Higborn human can shadow their own self from another Highborn." Malkai said. "Even if it's only for a few seconds. Ah, it's so good to see you too, little brother. How long has it been, eh? Two decades? Three, maybe?"

Shormai shook his head comically and smirked. "A decade and a half, brother. A decade and a half. Then again, lifetimes can fly past us so fast we won't even notice. Kinda make me wonder what some Knife Ears think of us Highborns all the time, eh?"

Malkai scoffed. "Ah, enough with that talk. It can get you killed if any of the older Knife Ears hear what you say. As Highborns, we should never be arrogant to other races because we are naturally talented with

Light Magic. But in all reasonability, Knife Ears are born from the realm of Light Magic so we really can't compare our skills and abilities when it comes down to it, Shormai."

"Yes, can't compare, I agree. . .but this is the reason why I came here. To talk yes but, something direr. Importantly dire. . .to all Wirm. Even all Herta, if I have to say so myself." Shormai paused and looked behind his shoulder with squinted eyes. "As you said, we should never be **arrogant**, period. There's an evil plot at work and I need your help. Please, brother. No one can hear us speak. No one, understand?"

Growing up together, he knew if his brother was playing him for a fool like in old times. But this time, this was serious. He stared long and hard at Shormai with compassion, thought long but not too long to keep his brother waiting for a reply. With a exhale, he began. "Alright, Shormai. Don't worry, too. I cast a silencing barrier around the upper portion of the Blue Spire so no one for 1000 miles can hear us. Both Light Magic and Dark Magic users won't be able to break it."

"But. . .how. . .is that possible. . ." Shormai whispered.

"Don't whisper, speak." Malkai stood stern and spoke loud. "The only way the spell continues to work is if the individuals inside, that's us, continued to speak loud. It only lasts for 2 minutes so please speak surely and with haste, Shormai."

Taking deep breaths and drilled his mind 7 times over and over. Shormai then began. "Right, loud. Got it. Whew. Someone plans on using Himortorian technology to conquer all of Wirm. I don't know who's behind this plot but I do know this. The group who have such interest in doing this call themselves the Disciples of Ga. I was able to squeeze an informant I managed to capture. All the informant's messages led back to. . .here. The leader of this group also states in his messages that he takes refuge at the Artifactorium. It's someone within the Artifactorium. I think. . .I think the Scorned are also assisting this person they call the Gavir. And if my memory serves me well, the word *gavir* is Horian in origin, meaning librarian. This fanatic leader must have a deep fascination with the entire lost culture as a whole. The messages prove it enough, at least. I sent two of my best assassins to eliminate this leader and all that came back was their heads."

"What do you ask of me, Shormai?" Malkai needed to know what his brother was trying to get at because the spell was starting to deteriorate. "What do you ask?"

"I need the best archeologists you can give me, brother. The messages never mention any locations or dig sites but specific landmarks. . .definitely. Like the Hush'a'Moon Mountains. I can barely make out letters in the Himortorian language or even operate Himortorian technology safely and survive. Your students, however, are young archeologists, who have seen and been around Himotorian tech and even operated some of their vehicles too."

"They're still young, Shormai!" Malkai insisted. "They're not warriors or heroes like the ones you hire from your local inn! They are practically still teenagers. I won't allow it, brother."

Shormai disappointedly nodded. "Please, brother! Lend me your best! You don't know the level of insanity these maniacs have with them. I have seen what they can do. They will stop at nothing to get what they want!"

"All the more reason to say no to your request, brother." He shot back. "You know better than anyone here why I can't allow that."

Shormai scoffed."What? The Chantel Incident? So what! You and I know it wasn't our fault those young archeologists died. The cavern was marked as **cleared**. Cleared, I tell you."

Silence fell upon the two siblings as their quarreling ceased, both staring at each other intensely with only half a minute remaining.

"Eslamai died trying to stop Disecples of Ga," Shormai said, causing Malkai's mouth to open at this sudden, grieving news. Shocked and saddened beyond belief, Malkai turned his head and halted the oncoming tear that wanted to force its way out of his eye. Shormai could see how much this pained him. "She died knowing that we'll never let her death go unpunished. We're supposed to carry on the good fight, no matter the cost. I guess you have forgotten the promise you made that day, brother." He said, then with a swift turn he walked towards the opened doors.

In all his years, this is the second time in history that he is ever going to agree with his brother. *Father forgive me*, Malkai thought. "Alright, alright. I'll do it, Shormai."

"You will?" Still facing the doors, Shormai was hesitant to confirm his brother's words. "Your sure, Malkai?"

Malkai made a displeased face. "Only once more. Once more. I can't bare to imagine what harm will come to them, but I am allowing this only once more." He turned to the window, seeing the beautiful and glorious sun today that shined into his office, calming his spirit. "But you have to promise me, Shormai. Promise me this, please. You'll do everything in your power to make sure that no harm comes to them. Please promise me this."

Assuring his understanding of the situation they were both in, he slowly nodded to his older brother. "I will do everything in my power to protect them. Even if it means. . . giving my own life for theirs."

The Hush'a'Moon Mountains

A tale of betrayal and loyalty, peace over war, and magic-binding secrets that will last generations to come. Even love. The public knows barely any history of these mysterious mountains, for much hysteria and conspiracy surrounds the Hush'a'Moon Mountains and the battle that happened there. Although generic but still carried significant meaning throughout the centuries across the Kingdom of Melek, the War For Hush'a'Moon Mountains was a long and bloody civil war between the mountain natives known simply as the **Mountain Folk** and Knife Ear militaristic explorers titled **Heimein's Troop**. Rumored as being the first humans who settled into the country before the Kingdom of Melek along with its surrounding provinces, were even established. As their name implied, the Mountain Folk built many suspended villages that hung on the various peaks, cliffsides, and clifftops. From what the written historical document suggests, mistaken at first glance by Heimein's Troop as dragon nests, swearing even to themselves that their Knife Ears eyes were deceived by what they saw in front of them. This led many historians and archeologists to concur that even Knife Ears as a race had, without a doubt, better-than-human vision. Historical evidence also confirms that Knife Ears could see the most minute details on the tiniest insects of Wirm, can spot a single dull rock on a mountainside riddled with hundreds of trees and. . .in their own words, *countless universes concealed within a single teardrop*. With Heimein's Troop themselves confirming in their writings that what they saw had the appearance of dragon nests, also confirms that the Mountain Folk had either a very superior form of camouflage or they used Dark Magic to keep their entire villages hidden from vicious predators like the Cliff Crawlers. After Heimein's Troop made a sturdy outpost in between the mountains, they finally received orders from their chief director, who remained in their homeland. Kingdom of Silvendir.

Captain Avela Firm's orders read: You are to annihilate any of the natives if they show signs as Dark Magic users. Necromancy, Pseodo-Scimce, and Vampirism. Claim any land the natives are willing to part with. If none cooperate, wipe them out. If they show great resilience too much for your forces to handle Captain., retreat back to our kingdom to regain strength and regain numbers to conquer these lands. Also, the mountains you described in your earlier messages. . .our great and lustrous ruler, High Princess Daplhin has taken great interest in what lies beneath the mountains. Do not fail our kingdom and our final ruler.

This is your final order. Do not fail me, captain.

Merja Clemsen

Chief Director of the Expoloarty Division of Silvendir, Military Branch

But even after receiving this order, Captain Avela remained secretly neutral in carrying out this command. None of her fellow soldiers got the order, nor did her most trusted lieutenant. She kept it to herself and herself alone. Instead, she told her fellow soldiers that they will be ordered to make peace with the Mountain Folk and investigate further into the mountains themselves for Himortorian ruins. Mainly their obscure technology. But after a couple of years of *non-hostile* settling, 400 Knife Ears Sun soldiers marched from the Kingdom of Silvendir across the barren ice wastes of Misu, to finally the mountainous country of Melek. The very same country that Heimein's Troop was supposed to claim for the High Princess Daplhin. A long civil war began after Mountain Folk sympathizers(Knife Ears who were still loyal to Captain Avela and the Mountain Folk) who were only a handful of Knife Ears. Lasting for 5 years straight, the Sun soldiers finally defeated the Mountain Folk, along with Captain Avela and her beloved. Driving the surviving Mountain Folk into the lower mountains cave systems. To this day, many theories have been made about why High Princess Daplhin took an interest in the Hush'a'Moon Mountains or more specifically, what was supposedly underneath them. This civil war happened during the end of the 6th Era of Herta.

"You know, Daplhi. . ." Arcemo had a small book in her hand titled: *Battles on Hush'a'Moon Mountains: Notes and Messages.* She roosted herself comfortably on the window sill of the dormitory she shared with Jorka, Untha, and Daplhi. Dangling and swaying her feet over the edge of the window sill, sighing with pleasing comfort. Feeling the sun on her skin never felt so good. It is growing warmth and healing light felt like home to her. Raising her left leg and rubbed her smooth skin, massaging it at some points. "You don't know what you're missing! The suns feels so good."

"You do realize that our dorm is 50 feet off the ground, right?" Daplhi ensured, her eyes focused on the sketchbook while she lay lazily on her bed, rhythmically moving her legs back and forth in a playful manner. She liked to wear black socks and black tight, her green-dyed hair strands across her face. Resting her chin on her left palm and hummed a soft tune her parents used to sing to her before on long trips across the small province of Vilmir, within the Kingdom of Silvendir. "But hey, who am I to say what's dangerous to you, eh Arcemo?"

"I know how high we are, silly." Arcemo turned her head to Daplhi, almost halfway between a squeal and a laugh. Sighing as she looked back to her book. "It's just that, being this high and everything. It. . .reminds me of the cliffsides I used to spend my spare time at a lot. You know, back home. Listening to the crashing waves against the base of the cliffsides, petting pinch crabs, and even the smell of freshly chopped palm tree." She stared. . .stared at the surrounding forest, just outside the Artifactorium's stone walls. Remembering home and her family. "Back home."

Daplhi stopped in her sketch, noticing Arcemo's leaned posture. "You miss home, don't you? Forgive me! If I have stepped on something personal-"

"No, no. It's all right." Arcemo scooted her butt back from the windows sill's edge and into the dormitory's wooden floor. She faced herself where Daplhi lay and continued to read the book she selected earlier on her way from the library. "It's good that I miss home. I mean, look at me! No matter where I go I always carry home with me. Spiritually, of course."

"Spiritually. I wish I can be as spiritual as you, Arcemo." Daplhi said. "Oh, how I wish to be attuned with my god like you are too. That's what you said right? You're attuned with your god because. . .?"

"Hmm?" Arcemo chirped, taking a sip of water from her glass cup. "Oh, yeah of course. In fact, we as Sadyks believe that all people were created by a single god, each person spiritually connected to Him."

"What's his name again?" Daplhi asked. "Your god's name?"

"Usami the First Father." Arcemo felt chills throughout her body. "That's his name. Some people call him Yahmark, others call him Jen'tor or Bis but his true name is and should be Usami. My father and mother taught me since the first words I spoke as a baby."

"Cool." Daplhi rested her chin on both her hands and listened with awe. "Kinda reminds me of the battle that occurred on Hush'a'Moon mountains. One of the key reasons why the natives fought for their home for so long was because they weren't willing to bow down to the Knife Ears god. They believed only in one god but the Knife Ears were like *we don't care if you got a god already. We got better weapons and better manners so that makes us naturally superior and better than all of you!*" Daplhi imitated a Knife Ear aristocrat from a theatre play she remembered watching when she was 5 years old. Waving her arms about ridiculously causing her and Arcemo to giggle. "Goes to show. People will think highly of themselves just because they think they are. Forcing religions and hostile takeover of land. I'm just glad the old monarchy is done away with, honestly. With our new king installed upon the throne, I see a bright and peaceful future for not just Knife Ears but for all races on Wirm."

Arcemo sat next to Daplhi on her bed, crisscrossing her legs, and shrugged funnily about the old Knife Ears way of life. "As much as I like to think that the Knife Ears conquered the mountains because of that, I did some extensive research on the Sun soldiers battalion, the chief director in charge of Heimein's Troop expedition, Captain Avela herself, and even the true nature behind the Mountain Folk themselves."

Bring herself up to chest level so she can see what Arcemo was reading. She sat herself up and sat right next to Arcemo, examining what section of the book she was at. The two have grown very close since their first archeological expedition together alongside Mirk as a head archaeologist. Since this was the female dormitory, they spent most of their time together drawing maps, studying languages, occasionally sparring with each other, and doing some symbolic programming, creating tiny contraptions out of wood and stone. Since Daplhi was a Knife Ear, barely turned 18, and grew up in the rougher parts of the province of Vilmir. Being a country girl, she didn't mind Arcemo's company at any day and any time.

"Really?" Daplhi asked, scooting closer and closer, filled with curiosity. "What are you getting at, then?"

"My personal theory states that the true reason why High Princess Daplhin insisted for the mountains to be taken over is. . ." Arcemo reached for a small notebook, in her hanged-up backpack near her own bed. Upon opening, Daplhi could not believe her eyes. She wrote over 500 pages worth of personal research, notes, and study.

"Is because what, Arcemo?" Daplhi insisted. "Is because of what? Dark Magic maybe or perhaps even a dragon-worshiping cult! I read in a couple of history books that Knife Ears during the time eradicated all kinds of cults!"

"Himortorian artifacts, that's why," Arcemo said. "Along with an intact underground structure built by the Himortorians. It was gigantic too! Its entire circumference was larger than Morvick City! Which in total, is 70.2km!"

Resting on her shoulders, she tilted her head and said. "Where did you read this from? What evidence do you have to support your **cool** theory? Not saying that I don't believe you or anything, given how many archeological discoveries you made over your time here at the Artifactorium! You are super intelligent and kind. Don't get me wrong, no one should question your credibility."

Arcemo smiled and flipped to a part in her notebook where it had detailed drawings and rough sketches of the supposed structure underneath the Hush'a'Moon Mountains, half a mile underground. "I understand. Here." She passed the drawing to Daplhi. She examined the drawing closely. "I got this drawing off a wandering trader who claimed he saw it himself. He said that the six inward arches somehow kept a miniature sun in the center, taking away all weapons that he and his friends carried, and consuming them into its blue light. And look, look, look! The dirt smudges at the bottom of the drawing. I did some testing and guess what?! It's dirt that can't be found anywhere else on Wirm! How cool is that, Daplhi!"

"Spectacular!" Daplhi held her tongue and thought before continuing. "It's just that, you know. . .certain people here actually don't believe your expertise in being an archeologist. A certain someone among them being *Jorka*."

Jorka wasn't the kindest person towards Arcemo during her time here, always trying to prove something, always trying to be better than. . .well. . .anyone here. It's just hallway talk but there are rumors that Jorka might have a thing for Mirk, it's just that she never opens up herself in that manner. It's not her fault, of course. Highly speculative, but Horians born with certain names become their names. Jorka in Horian language means *rude but can understand others*. Figures, eh?

Arcemo's shoulder shrugged about Jorka. "I know what Jorka thinks about me. I mean. . .who wouldn't? I came from an island out in the middle of the ocean, ignored and believed to be completely savage. I could correct them, but what difference would one Sadyk make now? So

I told myself and my parents, I have faith as a Sadyk, that with humility and integrity as an archeologist, I will make sure that we as a race on Herta, deserved to be heard and will be remembered throughout history as not a proud, not a violent, not a dumb but a humble race that could accomplish anything. A humble race."

Arcemo could feel Daplhi teared up from her inspiring words and turned to see her rubbing her left eye, her elongated ears lowered in a saddened position. Her teared-up eyes gleamed in the light as she jolted to Arcemo and gave her a tight hug. Arcemo's eyes shot open at her doing this, but as a Sadyk and a Cloud, she could understand why. "Oh, Arcemo. Next time when you are going to be emotional, please warn me. I get very emotional, you know. Very emotional."

As Arcemo returned the hug, she couldn't help but feel grateful for the connection she had with Daplhi. The two of them were from different worlds, but they shared a deep respect and admiration for each other's cultures. It was moments like this that reminded Arcemo of the importance of understanding and compassion in a world that often felt divided.

After a few moments, Daplhi pulled away and wiped her eyes with the back of her hand. "I'm sorry," she said, her voice cracking slightly. "It's just...your words touched me deeply. As a dark-skinned Knife Ear, I sometimes feel like we are misunderstood by others. But you...you have always been so open-minded and accepting."

Arcemo smiled, feeling a warmth in her chest. "I just believe that someday, we can all learn from each other," she said. "Our differences are what make us unique, but our similarities are what bring us together."

Daplhi nodded, a small smile playing on her lips. "You're right," she said. "I'm grateful for our friendship, Arcemo. And in a way, you inspire me to be a better person."

"Well, good thing I'm an empath," Arcemo said, her left ear twitching slightly from the noise she heard on the bottom floor, down the stairs. "I hear someone coming up the stairs." She turned her head in the direction of their dorm door.

With her magnified hearing as Knife Ear, she could make each and every step up the stairs. Disconnecting her wrap from Arcemo kindly, and could make out the figure of who was coming up the stairs. It was Horian for sure, but the horns weren't proportionate from each other. This could only mean. . .

"HEY YO!" Jorka shouted before slamming the door wide open. "You two, come with me."

"Why?" Daplhi asked, slipping on her leather boots. "Did something happen?"

"Nothing happened, stupid," Jorka said. "Today apparently is the day, Arcemo."

"One of Arcemo's Himortorian artifacts activated!" Jorka said. "Mirk and Bargas are already down at the Undergo Vault investigating what's going on. So come on stinky feet, we have no time to waste!"

"Right, Jorka!" Arcemo chirped, hopping on both feet, dusting off herself, and stuffing her small notebook back into her backpack. "Come on, Daplhi, let's go!"

The Undergo Vault

Certain shadows tend to disturb Mirk from time to time, especially down here in some of the unlit rooms of the Undergo Vault. The inspired catacomb-like architecture of the vault reminded Mirk of the history books that deep-dived into its making. Taking over 2000 years to build, with rooms spanning millions of miles underground and 12578 miles directly below the Artifactorium's foundation. Now. . .some would admit to its glorious splendor because of the almost infinite amount of artifacts that have been collected era after era. But why so much in a place that can only be visited by archeologists(including allowed citizens or high royalty figures)? Well, it is said by some of the teachers at the Artifactorium that certain artifacts stored in the Undergo Vault are there because they are *potentially dangerous to not just Herta, but the whole universe*. In the corner of his eye, a small shadowy figure crossed pillars, following both Bargas and Mirk eerily and creepily. At least to Mirk's vision of course. He swore to himself that whatever or whoever was following them down here in the Undergo's long hallways. . .was definitely unnatural in origin. He could sense its beady eyes precariously staring at them, unnerving Mirk greatly. His twitched from what he thought was a slender hand that gripped his shoulder, making him gasp with fear, and, as a **natural** reaction, unhooked his crossbow and aimed behind him.

Mirk's heart was pounding as he tried to keep his eyes focused on the shadowy figure that seemed to be following him and Bargas. As he raised his crossbow, he could feel the weight of it in his hands. He had been trained to use it in case of any danger, but he never thought he would have to use it in the Undergo Vault of all places. The eeriness of the situation made him wonder if he was hallucinating or if there was something truly dangerous lurking in the shadows.

"What's eating you?" Bargas halted in his tracks as he saw Mirk take a defensive position with his weapon. "This is like the fourth time you stopped because you thought you saw something down here! Now look, the glow worm lamp is starting to go out." Bargas held in his right hand a cylindrical device, four glass holes revealing inside a large blue glow worm that wiggled slowly. Its body's natural light started to fade, causing the lamp's light to fade also. He shook it slightly to bring back the light.

Mirk stared longed into the dark, slowly holstering his crossbow, and sighed. "Don't you feel like there's something watching us when we're down here? I mean, really? I am starting to think that the Undergo Vault is inhabited by the Shadow Dwellers or something."

As Mirk's words echoed through the silent underground chamber, a chill ran down his spine. He couldn't shake the feeling that they weren't alone. The Undergo Vault was said to hold ancient treasures, but it was also rumored to be cursed. The hairs on the back of Mirk's neck stood on end as he strained his ears, trying to hear any sound that might confirm his fears once again. And then Bargas slapped on the back of his head. "Ow!"

"Quit being paranoid about this place and get back to searching for where Arcemo's artifact floated off too, okay, Mirk?" Bargas kinda had Mirk's collar in his grasp as he walked, almost dragging because of how hysterically he was beginning to sound. It annoyed him. "You know, Mirk, why is it when we always come down here you start acting like this?"

"We usually come down here with an older archeologist at least," Mirk stated, checking left and right for any movement. "Who had experience traversing these ever-changing tunnels? Do you remember the pattern in whence they change right, Bargas?!"

"SHHHHHHHHHHHHHHH!" Bargas yanked him silly, his nostrils flaring as his eyes beamed with frustration from Mirk's incompetence. "I remember the pattern, Mirk. Too well, to say the least. Look, see this tunnel in front of us? It would shift 45 degrees north the moment we walked through it, taking us back to the elevator shaft from where started. To our right, leads to a section solely committed to Knife Ear artifacts dating back to the 5th Era of Wirm."

Mirk, straightened his posture and calmed his mind, remembering the different tunnelways and hallways that led to the multiple rooms filled with artifacts of old. The timed pattern in which also the Undergo Vault's tunnelways shift every hour or triggered step."To our left, is where the Gorgmorian artifacts remain. But the hallway would have closed in behind us if continued in that direction. Whew, it's all coming back now."

"You see?" Bargas raised the lamp to head level now, its blue light shining their path ahead. "You keep getting spooked we won't be able to find Arcemo's artifact and put it back. Now come on, let's go! And for the last time. . ." Bargas turned his head slowly, continuing to walk into the darkened hallway where three shadowed silhouettes crept closer and closer toward him. "There is no such thing as Shadow Dweller-AAAAHHHHHHMYGOSH!!" Bargas high pitch scream from whatever he saw made Mirk jump with his returned fear.

"AAAHHHH!" Unhooking his oakwood crossbow(No bigger than his forearm) so fast, the holster flew off into the shadows, never to be found again. He aimed down his sights on whatever scared Bargas. But what he saw next with his keen Knife Ear vision caused his heart to drop. "No, what is it?!?!"

"Eeek!" Whapam! A solid fist squashed Bargas's nose, causing him to stagger in his stance, and with his left hand holding it up stop the bleeding. He groaned from the rising pain Jorka's punch gave him. He knew how strong Horians were too, so it just fed the rising pain. "Bargas! Big dummy! You know how I am when people sneak up on me like that!"

"Jo-ka!" His voice muffled, barely being able to talk from the blood in his nose. "You hit me in the snoz! The snoz, Jorka!" Still holding the lamp in hand, kneeling down on the floor. He groaned loudly as he prepared himself for what he was going to do next. Then. . . Crack! "Oh! Thank the gods I was able to fix my nose!"

"You dummy!" Thinking Bargas was being a big child, in her own eyes, either always exaggerated or always crying. Being herself as always, she kindly approached to examine how serious the bleeding was. Apparently, this wasn't even the worst injury Bargas sustained during his time here at the Artifactorium. Sure most of his injuries were minor sword gashes, scrapes on his arms, and intense bruising from his self-commenced fistfights he did with **his own words** indecent men who had no manners or respect for others. These fistfights were usually done between him and some bandit, mercenary, scoundrel, or criminal that he came across in long archeological travels across the Kingdom of Melek. Which is surprisingly quite often, to say the least. Even though he is of the Horned Race, he wasn't born in the mushy marshlands of the Horned Empire. No, instead his parent migrated from their homeland and settled in the Kingdom of Melek. "Hmmmm. . . well, I can say this, Bargas. Your nose definitely is not bleeding anymore. I'll say that. But just to be doubly sure. . .Daplhi! Use your Knife Ear magic to heal whatever might be still damaged in his nose."

Daplhi stuck out her tongue mockingly and walked with her arms close to her sides to go heal her injury-prone friend. "Come on, let me see if the spell still works." Placing her gloved hand on his nose gently, she recounted the healing spell that her parents have taught her as a child. She closed her eyes before announcing the spell. *"Ahmer Zoser Vanos!"* A flash of yellow light spiraled around his head, feeling the pain from his nose vanish completely. Daplhi removed her hand and nodded to him to give a-okay sign.

He made three sharp inhales, just be sure. "Thanks, Daplhi. I owe you one."

Booping him in the nose, smirking as she did so. "You know you owe me more than just that, Bargas. How many times have I patched you up by now? Because I can tell you this, it's definitely more than 20 if that's what you're about to say." She opened her waist satchel, revealing a bunch of cookies she stored away in times just like these. Twindling her fingers to choose which one he should get, she decided to hand one of the larger cookies to Bargas, insisting that he'd take it or else she give it to Jorka. She baked the batch just this morning too, so they still had the fresh taste to them. It was everyone's favorite too: Chocolate Chip. "Your lucky I even know that healing spell. I could only imagine what you'd look like if hadn't kept up with your physical condition."

Jorka chortled. "He'd look like a beaten pile of Nomar fruit balls if you ask me!" Nomar fruit balls to Horians were a medley of mulched fruits that consisted of apples, grapes, bananas, grapefruits, avocado, and pineapple. Stirred continuously until the mixture is unrecognizable as a fruit mix. Color varies depending on the amount. Then shaped into small balls and baked in the oven for about 2 minutes. Cevil Nomar is the Horian that made this recipe on his travels to the Bridge Islands. It is considered a certain delicacy to much of the Horned Race. To other races, however, it is seen as something you feed farm animals.

Mirk stood there staring at Jorka, disgusted by the image that Jorka planted in his imagination, making him shake his head as lowered his crossbow. "That's not something I'd want to see in real life."

"Look, guys! As we exited the elevator, this artifact I found ran immediately for my arms!" Arcemo said happily, holding the Himortorian artifact in her iron grasp. "Good thing Daplhi and I were just in time to grab the silly thing. It barely gave us any fuss, too. Right, Daplhi?"

"I *know*, Arcemo," Daplhi agreed, clipping her satchel's lock. "But one thing that I don't get is why it didn't just teleport out of here like last time?"

It had multiple mechanical arms built into it, each with miniature three-fingered hands and a circular cute, frowning face engorged into its spherical body. Its arms flailing about in an attempt to escape from Arcemo, but knowing how Sadyks are, once she had her grip on something, she wasn't planning on letting go. The green eyes it had was similar to rare gemstones found in deep caves all across Wirm, mainly in the What was really interesting though about this artifact is that it had the innate ability to travel to exact locations in an almost instantaneous fashion, similar to telesphere technology developed by the Horned Race. To the others, the idea of this *thing* has a mind of its own, kind of creeped them out a bit.

"Maybe it wants to be with us!" She raised the Himortorian artifact to her chest, hugging it tightly, and rubbed it on its cold metal forehead. Causing it to vibrate, matching her gentle heartbeat. To Jorka and Mirk, it sounded awfully like a house cat purring, a metallic undertone. "I mean if it really wanted to leave this place, it really can! But no! It wants to stay here. If I recall, the only areas I remember it teleporting to our dorms. As if it's playing hide and seek with us!"

"Well, it does behave like a pet, that's for sure," Mirk said. "And it definitely is not scared of us at this point. I wonder what function did this serve though when the Himortorians were alive. Hmm, I wonder. . ."

"Uh, excuse me!" Shouted Jorka, leaning her hand on a nearby wall that led to the Himotorian section of the Undergo Vault, where the artifact is supposed to be on display and contained. Straightening her leather jacket, her fingers lined her circular collar and blew some strands of her hair that blocked her view. "Can I be the one to point out that this Himortorian artifact is one of the few that still functions and operates on its own? Sure, most of their terrestrial and aerial vehicles still work, but as far as the Artifactorium having a great supply of *working automaton*s, that's a big no-no." Placing a hand on her right hip, she continued to look at the automaton Arcemo held in her arms like a sleepy cat. "Well, this artifact is one of the exceptions."

Bargas wiped off whatever leftover crumbs were on his face, releasing a small burp. "Don't mean to sound *rude*, Arcemo, but where did you say you found this artifact again?"

Rubbing its metal head ever so gently, bringing it to her chest closer. "Near a camp trail at the Hush'a'Moon Mountains. When I was walking the trail, I noticed a faint glint of the golden metal that Himortorian artifacts are made of. It was buried by a foot of dirt, so the only thing I could see was its legs popping out of the ground."

"Let's, not dilly dally, my friends," Mirk said, pointing to the Himortorian display room. "We came down here with a single purpose: to apprehend whatever artifact that was causing all the ruckus down here in the Undergo Vault. Not saying that Acremo's artifact caused any damage but still, we are going to fulfill our jobs as archeologists of the Artifactorium and put it back where it belongs."

"Ha!" Bargas barked. "You know, technically in our culture, the artifact should belong where it was found. And it was found in the dirt at the Hush'a'Moon Mountains. Just saying."

Jorka crossed her arms disapprovingly at her fellow Horian, looking at him with squinted eyes. "Well, duh, doofus. But we are not in Horned Empire and Mirk, Daplhi, and Arcemo aren't even Horian, so that means our customs. . .dosent fall upon them, Bargas."

He shot up his arms in a humorous, having a goofy expression to ensure his point. Since Bargas and Jorka were some of the only young Horians in the Artifactorium that came from the Horned Empire, following tradition and customs was key to Horned Race culture. Spanning over 16093440 kilometers with their capital stationed in the Upper Lands of Wirm, their empire to this day is one of the only ruling powers that hasn't fallen to political corruption during ancient times. Why? A successful bloodline of wise monarchs, that kept tradition and followed their customs. "Once again, just saying."

"I agree," Arcemo said, placing the spiderlike automaton near her bare feet. With its metallic purring, rubbing its head on her smooth legs. "Tradition is a key important thing to any race, even the traditions." Sighing, putting her feet inward slightly. "If only more people respected one's culture and history, Wirm would have probably ended up differently than it is now."

Mirk just stared blankly at everyone. "Let's just get this artifact back to where it belongs. Okay?"

The Lost Children

Written by Basagi Nomar, a Horian archeologist during the 7th Era

In all my travels across Wirm, the interconnected stories of the Lost Children(Possibly not literally.) always seemed to intrigue me, never losing my interest one bit. Now throughout Wirm's history, there have been many, many detailed accounts from the continents' natives that there was once a group of children-like people that came to Wirm in search of this unknown mineral called Aplatie. Aplatie, in the native stories, is always mentioned as glowing and never lost its luster. What is intriguing about this though is the mention of these children people in their stories and why they were searching for this mineral. From what the stories describe them looking like, having yellowish-brown skin and elongated limbs, that in the native's words, had large eyes like lizards. The Lost Children are also described as being confused-looking or always stumbling around, short-statured like a child. Hence, their name. The ancient natives of Wirm seem to have encountered these strange people multiple times in history, specifically the Tami tribe of the Upper Lands. I have spoken to the head chiefs over the years and each of them keeps telling the same story of the mysterious Lost Children. Yes, I know the language. Now, that being said, I have a number of theories on who these Lost Children are and why any of the many races of Wirm haven't come across or seen them since the Great Colonization. Keep in mind that all these stories that chiefs tell me seem to take place during the Great Colonization.

- **It is very possible that the Lost Children were descendants of the Himortorians. The yellowish-brown skin and their large lizard-like eyes were actually the golden metal armor that they wore. The lizard-like eyes were their strangely shaped helmets, adding to their almost obscure appearance. What strikes them off as not**

Himortorians is that they are explained as being tall as a child and their elongated arms, which historically known that Himotorians were taller than most humanoid races on Herta.

• They could possibly be just symbolic in meaning. Maybe the Lost Children could literally mean lost children that the natives had. A traumatic event maybe that happened to most if not, for some strange reason, all the native tribes on Wirm. The mention of the Lost Children always being confused or stumbling could represent that they were possibly suffering from a brain disease or illness that caused them impaired movement. The elongated limbs and lizard-like eyes could maybe be some form of deformity of the body. Still researching for clarity.

• This is a very loose but quite interesting theory but the Lost Children could very much be the Absolutes of old. It makes sense in a certain way because Absolutes are known to enwrap themselves with mortal shells to interact with the people of Wirm from time to time. In my studies, it appears that the Absolutes only came for a race that was in need of guidance, wisdom, knowledge, and understanding but very rarely interfered with mortal battles. But why would the Absolutes want a mineral?

• This theory is the least likely but the Lost Children could've been some of the voyaging Sadyks that came to Wirm during the Great Colonization. Highly unlikely again, because Sadyks have dark purple to very rarely bright pink hair with dark brown skin. None of them have elongated arms and none of them have lizard eyes. But the only reason why the Lost Children could have been the

Sadyks is because of the similar metal found on their island they call Sumb. The mineral glows and it can even absorb the sun's light. This could possibly mean that some Sadyks left their island in search of more of this rare mineral. Again, loose theory.

The Scorned

A soldier's hastily scribbled note was found on a blood-covered table at an outpost near the Horned Empire's border. It is about the Scorned's attack at her outpost, written during the Upper Land Wars in the 10th Era. The soldier in question is unknown and unnamed. All that is known of her is her age before she. . .disappeared. She was 26 it seems.

I am young and have forgotten my name. 26. I think. . .I don't have much time left. I feel. . .very dizzy. Getting difficult to. . .write. The Scorned. . .they broke into the first wall. Outside of our outpost has been taken over by the Scorned. I locked myself inside but. . .I don't think that will hold them for long. They were right outside, chanting. Just chanting. I need to stop them one way or another. The Himortorian. . .artifact here. . .must. . .hide it. They're telling me to let them in. Scratching and clawing. The Scorned. . .must. . .stopped. I have cut by one. . .their blades. I feel it's poison changing me as I write. Even now, my clothing rips and tears as if I am growing larger than my comrades. My muscles ache, my mind spins and my heart feels faint. My armor rusts when I touch it, I can't even fit my boots on anymore. I can barely speak. They. . .did. . .this to me. They made. . .into what I'm. . .becoming now. I will stop them, I must stop them. Their chanting. . .must be stopped. They. . .telling me. . .let them in. Never, maybe. No. Fear them! They are not to be trusted! They are the enemy! I am Scorned!

Searching for over 5 hours at this outpost for any surviving soldiers who were all posted here, General Pickit along with his specialized units of warriors gifted to him by the Knife Ears known as Sun Warriors found nothing. Nothing but this note and a piece of severed piece of a Scorned's ear. To this day, the soldiers and the Himortorian artifact were never found.

Gods of Herta So Far. . .

Yahmark: Known to the eastern humans as Bis or Jen'tor, revered by most humans as the divine creator of Existence, the Universe, and all of Herta. Morvick City has a giant statue dedicated to his entire being and is seen as the top of any pantheon. Highborns also believe in him, but revere him differently than other human races on Wirm. Being described as the pinnacle of fatherly love to his children, his true appearance takes the form of a red-eyed, dark-skinned bearded human, dawning magnificent blood-red armor, and is truly omnipotent.

Vtegu the All-Mither: In Knife Ear religion, the word *mither* means benevolent one. Depicted most of the time as a being made of pure starlight, her eyes being like the Great Suns and her dress made of endless clouds in historical paintings of her. Her people's belief in her gives her existence and with her power, she can supposedly change the fate of living creatures on Herta. In many cultures, Vtegu is also associated with the moon. Some believe that she is the goddess who oversees the phases of the moon, while others see her as a protector of those who journeys by night.

The Horned Race Pantheon of Gods

Zomriel the Flame: God of Fire and Change

Said to be the one who created the Great Suns of Herta, Zomriel lives in all fire and is the only god in the Horned Race pantheon that has no physical appearance besides his firey form. Representing the growing mountain of life itself, Zomriel can both appear as fierce, terrifying, or a docile meek little dwindling flame to his people.

Mosar the Undying: God of Death and Immortality

Known only for his place in the Horned Race afterlife as the Keeper of the Gate, King of the Dead, or Guardian of the Fallen. Mosar represents the end of all living things on Herta but also represents immortality to those who earned it. The Horned Race believes that if one dies in battle serving their monarch and lived their life with humility, Mosar will grant them immortality, unable of death ever again.

Ebibon the Fortress: Goddess of Strength and Power

Ebibon is known as the Goddess of Strength and Power to the Horned Race, representing qualities that embody perseverance and determination. Appearing as a 50-foot muscular female horian to her people every new year, wearing spiked armor that exposes her gigantic form, her bushy hair containing the deep forests of the known world.

Misar the Timeless: Goddess of Infinity and Perception

Misar is often depicted as a beautiful female horian with long, flowing hair and a serene expression on her face. Her horns were large enough to hold a small black moon on top of her head. She is usually shown wearing a flowing green robe, which symbolizes her infinite wisdom and knowledge.

The Sadyk Culture

Usami the First Father: Said to the true god of all, Usami the First Father is obscure as the people whom this god originated from. Since he came from the Sadyks, he is said to look like an elderly Sadyk, wielding a long wooden staff that at the head of it holds a small sun. His people worship him diligently and faithfully each and every day, including Arcemo. His worship is not just limited to the daily rituals, but also during significant life events such as births, weddings, and funerals. The small sun on his staff is believed to be a symbol of life and prosperity, and it is customary for the followers to offer fruits and flowers to it in order to seek blessings from the deity.

Note From The Author

Thank you for reading my story! I have some already published online if you are interested in reading more of my awesome stories, with more soon to be released to the public! Please, please share your constructive criticism of my books and others soon to come also. I am 18 years old(Just turned recently!) and being a writer is like literally one of my truest passions in life, second of course to be a good brother, son, and friend to my family and to the friends I have in the world. Check them out when you can! And remember, in the crude but honest reality we live in, we are bound by most of our physical potentiality as human beings. But fiction, allows us to expand our minds and our imaginations, making us truly boundless and free to a whole new universe of infinity!

SEARCH FOR THESE ONLINE NOW!

HOLYGUARD: A GALAXYSTAR STORY

2896: Interplanetary War: Capturing of General Philkus

2896: Interplanetary War: TYPHON

&

More GALAXYSTAR stories, fantasy stories, and short stories coming soon this year!

For information on the universes I create, please feel free to ask any questions in your review that you may have that need good explanations!

As a side note, I also draw my own book covers because I'm working on a tight budget that doesn't allow me to get a 30-day free trial. Jinkies. But anyhow, my sister does the coloring for most of my book covers!

Don't miss out!

Visit the website below and you can sign up to receive emails whenever Haviti Washington publishes a new book. There's no charge and no obligation.

https://books2read.com/r/B-A-NZTX-UAGIC

BOOKS2READ

Connecting independent readers to independent writers.